Haunting Tales of Tower Grove East

W. F. Gunn

ISBN: 979-8-694963-97-8

PREFACE

Over fifty-some years of living in the Tower Grove East neighborhood of South St. Louis, observing its ebbs and flows toward significance, the most challenging of times are when criminals perpetrate their nefarious deeds.

Of all the indignities villainy visits upon its victims, among the deepest is a sense of helplessness—of not being able to stop or undo the harm . . . or see justice.

That is why I conceived of a literal way to turn the tables on criminality. I invented a supernatural superhero, one with offbeat powers that hunts evil. My superhero is ancient and big. Very big. 326 acres big.

It is the Tower Grove East Neighborhood of South St. Louis, Missouri. Not just its people, but the primordial place itself, where terror becomes terrified, where crooks and miscreants get unexpected comeuppance, and good is the natural order.

Over the years, I wrote these tiny stories every Halloween. Each inspired by outrage on social media over porch pirates, car thieves, litterers, et al. That, and memories of *Twilight Zone, Tales from the Crypt* and *Outer Limits.*

I recommend parental guidance on all the stories in the collection, except for one. Chapter 13, the final chapter, is for all ages. In each account, cathartic intervention on behalf of decency happens with ferocious finality.

Horribly written to warn whatever bad-to-the- bone evil thinks it can cross our threshold without consequences . . . our cosmic fly traps await.

W. F. Gunn

CONTENTS

The Haunted Lake

Origin

Out of the firmament, a meteor cut through the cosmos straight toward a very young Earth. The fireball pierced our infant planet like a hypodermic, plunging deep into the marrow of Earth's iron soul to inject its passenger.

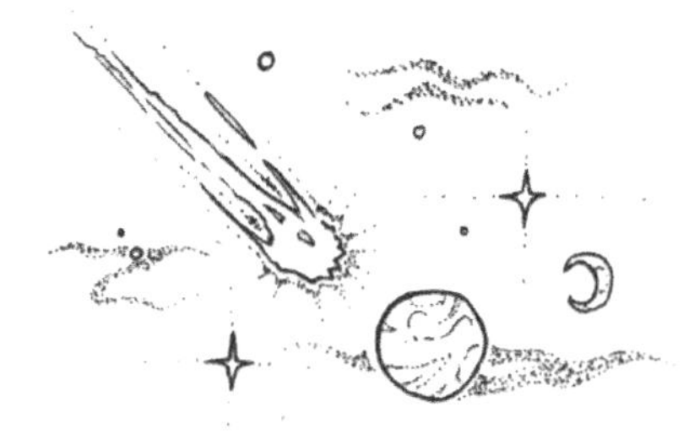

Entombed in molten minerals for a billion years, essence liquefied; it waited.

Then came the earthquake. A crack from sky to mantle split the continent, opening the iron crypt in which it slumbered. Up and out, it bubbled, in torrents, billions of gallons, in a wild drive to the surface, shooting into the air, where its great volume gathered and hovered above the land. In a slow, oozing collapse, it became a lake. Over millions of years, the great, placid vortex drew an abundance of flora and fauna.

Some drank and thrived, others not so much; those of vicious temperament, of madness, territorial or anti-social . . . all perished. The Osage tribe, well aware of its unearthly energy, kept a respectable distance from the lake but created a symbol for it and placed it upon their ancient amulets to repel evil.

The lake's first documented disturbance appeared in 1721 in the diary of a French lieutenant. His company's cruel captain took to berating a young soldier wounded in action. The captain waylaid the boy, kicked him, and beat him. He grabbed a stick and chased the unfortunate man toward the shoreline, away from the light of the campfire.

A bloodcurdling scream abruptly ended the assault. In seconds, the whole encampment arrived at the scene. They discovered the lad unconscious. The only sign of the captain lay in the very tip of the feather from his tall cap protruding from the muddy bank beneath which they found him upright.

Stories persisted as settlers surrounded the reservoir, converting prairie and woods into farms, followed by the city of St. Louis spreading westward to the sounds of hammers and picks, wagons, and mules. Oral histories of the lake passed superstitions through generations.

Eventually, residents established a companion graveyard overlooking the lake for protection in the afterlife.

The stories of gruesome endings for those deserving of it grew. The critters and characters of the once wild territory dwelled peacefully with occasional evidence of unwary wickedness.

1903 civilization came en masse, and as developers built the dwellings of Tower Grove East, the body of water withdrew and disappeared back into the land and lay suspended below its roads and living rooms.

That evanescence continues to prey on nastiness via earth and concrete, brick and asphalt, stone and wood, vegetation, creatures, and humans. They are alert; sentinels standing ready to terrify wrongdoers. It remains a place of comeuppance for evil as chronicled horrifyingly in these Haunting Tales of Tower Grove East.

1 MEAT ME IN ST. LOUIS

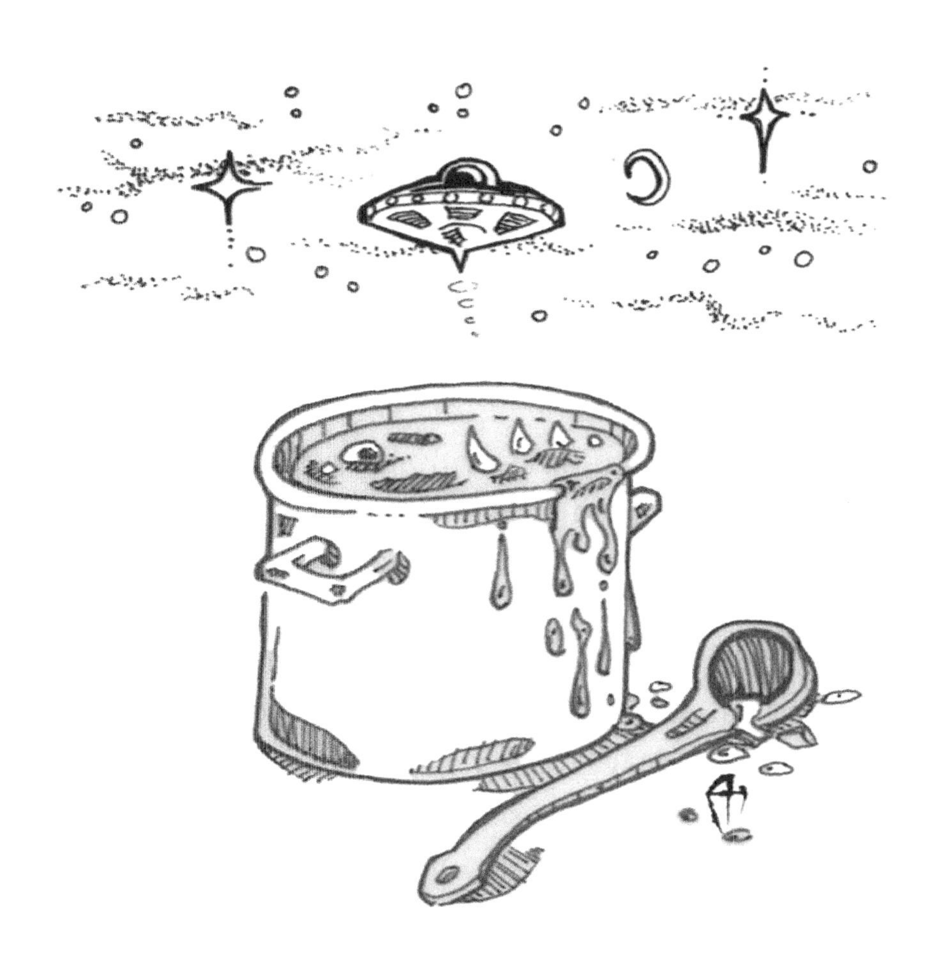

The two creatures stood facing each other, anger rippling through their bodies as each claimed discovery of the planet. Between them hovered a holographic globe—Earth. Images of various flora and fauna of the planet floated around it. The two creatures each gripped a singular image of a human, an intergalactic delicacy desired throughout the Universe.

A third creature appeared. It was larger than the other two and swatted the image away, drawing yellow blood from the two clenched fists. His dull, black, projecting teeth retracted.

"We share meat and credit," he growled. He turned to survey the spinning globe. Others swarmed about the giant, awaiting orders. Resolute, he pointed.

"We must sample the food before a harvest. I will go myself. Select a location while I prepare for materialization."

***

Blinks never gave his complete name. He would just tell you to call him Blinks, which he did—a lot. Blink, that is. He started work as a young boy at Henry Shaw's hardware store. He sharpened blades and became his burgeoning game hunter.

Shaw took a liking to him, eventually recruiting Blinks to join in on the creation of a botanical garden and park with neighborhoods expanding in every direction, especially east.

Henry Shaw died on a blistering hot day in August 1889. At his side, old Blinks nodded at each of the great man's last words. He demanded that Blinks swear allegiance to what would become the Tower Grove East neighborhood next to his park. The great man died before saying why. And so it was.

A sling blade strapped to his leg and a burlap sack over his shoulder prepared Blinks should he encounter a tasty morsel for dinner. He walked daily through the fields and woods of his adopted neighborhood. He cleared paths, chased off malcontents, and generally cared for the area like a doula assisting a birth.

The developers came. Up went homes and multi-family flats, yards, and streets. Blinks continued his patrol of Tower Grove East well into his hundredth year.

***

Relentless pursuit of food for his kind had forced the creature into materializing, into horrors his subordinates could not fathom. Since he was first to sacrifice when food was low, it was only just that he should feed first in a time of plenty. He salivated, thinking of the sour flesh of human meat, the most satisfying innards that pop and gush when eaten raw; the sweet newborn swallowed whole. Fermented human body hair, known for its reproductive stimulation, added great value to the harvest. He would ensure the manifest claimed a hairless harvest.

The creature violently collapsed its exoskeleton to become half its mass and crawled into the materializer, adjusted the restraints, and signaled for the transfer to begin.

It lowered several of its eyelids. The materializer dissolved it into particles of light waves streaking toward Earth for reassembly. It whipped through atmosphere over oceans, mountains, deserts, clouds, plains-lakes-fields-trees-dirt-dirt-dirt . . . rock.

***

Blinks sat in his kitchen, using the whetstone to caress the sling blade's cheeks. His time on Earth was near its end, and he would soon leave his beloved Tower Grove East to help Mr. Shaw cultivate Heaven.

A sudden sense that something was about to happen rushed through him. He had to get up—now! Had to go—now without knowing why or where. He adjusted his bib overalls, holstered his blade, gathered his burlap sack, and commanded his tired old legs to get moving toward the heart of Tower Grove East.

***

The creature's eyelids unfolded as it tried to expand its mass with much resistance. They had materialized him underneath the surface. This was no miscalculation—this was mutiny. Not knowing how deep he was, the creature burrowed upward, away from the gravity-shattering strata of the mantle he dug.

***

Blinks stopped at the intersection of Virginia and Pestalozzi Streets. The hair on the back of his neck stood on end. He blinked at the new brick streets, the freshly landscaped lawns, and fancy new streetlights glowing brighter as dusk deepened.

***

The creature's claws crushed rock, slashed clay, and sloshed through groundwater in a furious drive to the surface that promised sweet human flesh. A loud THUMP from below rocked a flower garden in a fenced backyard . . . then another thump . . . then another. Flowers fell, the soil beneath them crumbling and bubbling up, until the creature emerged. Its claws slowly extended, its body expanded, and it rose to its full height to survey its hunting grounds.

***

After taking a few cautious steps along Virginia, Blinks stopped. He lifted his head to listen to the wind and the sounds of the neighborhood. Beneath his feet, a tremble—to the left! Without hesitation, he turned and headed east down Pestalozzi Street, unholstering his sling blade and picking up speed until he was at a full run.

***

The creature's gut convulsed at the overwhelming smell of human. He ached to eat and never stop. An idea—stay and feed, self-replicate into a swarm with full control of the largest inventory of fermented human hair in the galaxy! It acted on impulse and sent a message: "URGENT! Meat contagion fatal! Am dying! You must escape—warn all!"

The creature's craft disappeared instantly from the stratosphere.

***

Blinks stopped, his gaze on the gangway between two buildings. Something, whatever it was, was in that backyard. Blinking rapidly, he sped through the dark canyon, his hand tight on his sling blade.

***

The creature sensed its prey—its first meal! Scanning the darkness, it rotated its head, then ceased when it saw its target. Usually skittish, stupid animals, this human walked directly toward him.

The creature released a terrifying sound—the human kept coming. It lunged forward and attacked its meat.

One fell swoop—THWACK!

***

Blinks pondered the thing for a moment. Then stuffed the halves into his burlap sack and slung it over his shoulder. He smiled and waved at strolling neighbors on his way back to his kitchen.

2 CAT NIP

Spring 1861. The moonless night and dark shadows hid the marauder as he watched the lawmen set up camp. He would wait to make his move. Bound for the Mississippi River a few miles east and lusting for gold carried by men well rid of it, he bided his time.

Last week, before he jumped and gutted a trapper, he made the man tell where he got the gold. The terrified man told of a riverboat what stops at St. Louis the first of every month. Traders bought his pelts on their way south. It was them that paid in coin and amber rock. It was them and their gold the desperado sought.

Travelers found the trapper, and the law had been tracking his killer for six days now across the Missouri hills to the Gateway to the West.

The marauder slipped like a ghost into their camp. He held his hand over one lawman's mouth and pushed his knife through muscle and artery till its sharp edge nicked the vertebrae at the rear of his throat. The second and third lawmen also died quietly in their bedrolls, which unnerved him. He had looked forward to the rush of resistance and, even more deliciously, to the inevitable begging.

Something stirred in the empty bedroll of his first victim. He approached it cautiously, and it stirred again. Out sprang a calico cat, and the bandit shot it square between the shoulders, severing its head from the writhing body.

The marauder departed the halo of the lawmen's fire. In the distance, another blaze caught his attention against the greater glow of St. Louis. Settlers, he thought. Easy targets, usually too scared to do anything but blubber. He would put the fear into them and rest the night with a woman, if there was one. Perhaps he'd kill them all after breakfast to get his blood up for the half day's travel to the riverfront.

With the help of an abolitionist contractor, slaves who purchased freedom in terrible ways bought a plot of land on which to build a house of their own. They chose the southern tip of a small lake at the quiet end of a cemetery in what would one day become the Tower Grove East neighborhood. The stout stone foundation would soon support six narrow rooms on two floors, with fat beams as sturdy as the family laboring to erect it.

The long day done, father and mother sat together by the fire to tend the youngest child beset with problems of the innards. Torch and bucket in hand, the older brother left to get water from the lake. The family's albino cat followed, but diverged toward the marauder.

The marauder flattened against the last tree before the clearing surrounding the construction site and closely watched the family. It wasn't uncommon for settlers to have a pistol or rifle close at hand. Suddenly, out of the dark woods to his left, an albino cat ambled across the clearing, headed straight for him. It paused halfway, checked on the boy and the family behind him at the fire, and continued toward the marauder. The cat stopped ten feet from the tree. With its colorless lips twitching in mute spasms, it peeked around the tree and trained its pink eyes on the robber.

"Git!" he said with hushed ferocity. "Git!" The cat sat down and, louder than the Marauder could have imagined, screamed, "OWWWW!" He dare not shoot it and sound an alarm. He reached for his long knife but had trouble sliding it out of its holster. The vines around the tree where he hid had tangled up in the hilt. He contorted to see it.

Something pierced his calf above his boot. He cried out in pain. Another stab on his other leg, and blood burbled and ran into the leather rim, warming his skin.

The marauder kicked violently at the unseen attacker but caught only air. He glanced up at the white cat sitting, staring at him. It let loose another, more menacing, "Owwwww!" Then another and another.

Against the guttural caterwauling, the marauder struggled to loosen the knife butt that held him fast to the tree as a deep gash opened across the back of his hand. He swatted at nothing.

Something razor-sharp sliced through his cheek and nose, another stroke slashed wide across his throat, and another snatched his right eye from its socket.

Unable to scream, he lashed out in a furious whirlwind of arms and legs. The slashing continued, eviscerating his abdomen, lacerating him from head to toe like an insane buzz saw, shredding his clothes, ligaments, and bones into a gooey mess.

A calico cat approached the albino, which hadn't moved. The calico sat and groomed itself in front of the white feline, and then the two companions walked through the darkness toward the firelight and family. As they strolled along, side by side, the clouds parted. Moonlight revealed only one cat walking alone—the albino.

3 GHOULING BANJO

The glockenspiel shipment from Munich arrived in Boston harbor as scheduled on February 5th. Management promptly warehoused it along with its companion cargo until the end of the workers' strike. The crate sat silently for nine months before its journey by rail to the Strassberger Conservatory of Music on the corner of Shenandoah Avenue and Grand Boulevard in St. Louis, Missouri. It was 1926, the year the Boston Banjo Murders ended.

The Banjo Murders dominated The Boston Globe's front page

for nearly six months. Readers absorbed chilling tales of barely audible banjo strings being plucked lightly just before each horrific murder. Dozens had fallen as the hushed, creeping carnage of the instrument felled them. Rumors persist to this day about two musicians, husband and wife from Appalachia, who appeared out of nowhere—Al, a guitarist, and his manager, Eve. They roared through Boston's music scene of flappers and high rollers. He carried among his several guitars a banjo case, although no one had ever seen the instrument or heard him play it.

Al and Eve Hallowed murdered for a living. He played music to relax between hits. A criminal faction in Boston called them up to eliminate an entire rival gang. They loved their work a bit too much and justified their propensity of giving their targets a gruesome end by believing their victims were all evil. As long as their marks satisfied their lust for blood, and plenty of it, they left the innocent alone.

Murder was a twelve-course meal for Eve; she favored her stiletto and collection of straight razors. Al liked to watch. The only tension in their lives came when there was a blood drought, and they were alone in the hills. The only human to slaughter being the other.

Their target that day was going to be easy: a disloyal security patrol at one of the dock warehouses. Al kept a black cloth over his banjo to keep it from catching light as he followed Eve. She could slink her way through the daylight. She signaled him to stay as she crept forward toward the guard. Her next signal would be for him to play.

Al didn't see it coming, not the signal or the sap that caught him just behind the ear. A silent trap, set and sprung, took Eve, too. Their employer didn't want to pay what he owed, so they had to die. He ordered Eve and Al dumped unconscious into an empty crate. The sealed crate muted the horror within as it awaited shipment.

Authorities never solved the Banjo Murders. With the prime suspects disappeared and no proof to pursue them, they closed the case.

In St. Louis, students and teachers eagerly waited for the Glockenspiel, which came late in the evening of October 31st. Upon opening the crate, they gasped in collective disbelief. It contained one banjo and two dead bodies. The Headmaster slammed it shut.

Police arrived on the scene, peeked inside, and resealed it until the detectives could examine it in the morning. The grotesque tableau of the fully dressed corpses of a man and a woman with dead hands around each other's throat in mutual strangulation horrified those who glimpsed it. Upset Strassberger devotees withdrew from the evening's Halloween festivities, canceled to the dismay of all. Except one, Gerhardt Gephardt.

At seventeen, he was the neighborhood tough guy. He did what he wanted when he wanted, and he wanted to go back to the Strassberger just before midnight and get a good look at the bodies.

He got in through the window near the boiler. Above it, a naked lightbulb scarcely cast enough light through the doorway and onto the box in the next room. Gerhardt entered the gloomy area. The crowbar used to open the crate sat where the police officer put it. The troublesome youth picked it up and pushed its flat end under the lid.

He pried, the lid squeaked, and he could have sworn he also heard a banjo twang. He moved farther along the seam and pried again. Then he distinctly heard a twice-plucked string. Gerhardt wrinkled his brow and before he could move the crowbar, the lid exploded off the crate.

The next morning, detectives found an empty crate and Gerhardt Gephardt, at least what they later identified as Gerhardt. Al and Eve were again free to prey together now . . . on evil in Tower Grove East. The slaughter of evil was as satisfying as the tender pluck of a banjo string, thanks to "Al Hallowed's Eve."

4 CHIN UP

George Gouache was a pale man, British by birth, brought to St. Louis by his parents. He relentlessly tried to distance himself from them to no advantage, since he lived in their basement. At twenty-nine years old, he had expenses, but absolutely no desire to work. His source of revenue was stealing cars. He fully assumed he would stop stealing them one day, get rich on his collection of American grunge, and move out. None of that mattered now, of course. He was a ghost; a ghost doomed for eternity to spook any would-be car thieves and stop sign runners away from the Tower Grove East neighborhood of South St. Louis.

George had a permanent assignment, the dead center of the intersection of Arkansas and Connecticut streets beneath asphalt, sewers, water lines, and dirt. He remained convinced the last car he stole before he died was abnormal. It was a set-up: window left open, keys in the ignition, packages in the rear seat, cassette tapes in the open; all too convenient. He should have sensed what was coming. But, once behind that wheel, the doors locked and there was no stopping it.

He and the car blasted through stop signs, ultimately hitting elderly twin brothers crossing the street. All three died in the crash. The brothers' ghosts stayed with George to oversee him for eternity. The brothers rather enjoyed having dominion over the hapless George; their heaven was his hell.

The brothers could sense when a car thief approached their territory long before George could. They would argue about the location of the target vehicle and often went on long rants in German, a sign George would soon be on duty and should adjust his head. You see, the crash had nearly severed George's head from his body. Though he used it to keen effect on car thieves and stop sign runners, the routine of it was bothering him.

For a very long time, he wanted to do something different to scare off bad guys instead of screaming and letting his head fall off to dangle by his vocal cords. It worked every time. But the whole nose-on-chest strategy was getting old. He needed to break the monotony. He tried holding his head in his hands while blathering and slobbering, but that seemed cliché. Consequently, George spent all his spare time thinking and thinking of how best to use his head. Deep down, he hoped he might somehow even get time off his sentence for creative initiative.

Suddenly, the brothers launched into a full-panic rush to get George to the surface and intervene in an imminent car theft that might cause a child harm. They now aimed their usual heated argument in German at George, who had no time to adjust his head onto his shoulders.

The would-be thief was not a pleasant person. There were plenty of good reasons for him to leave town, and in a hurry. He stalked the streets, looking for the right car to make his escape. Unknown to him, he had entered Tower Grove East, unfriendly territory for those with evil in their hearts.

The moonless night kept him from being seen, but it also made seeing difficult. He walked past one car after another, bowing slightly as he went to look for keys or door lock stems left up and unlocked. He thought he heard someone behind him and spun around. No one there.

He arrived at the corner of Michigan and Sidney streets, where a young couple and a small girl unloaded groceries from a double-parked car with the motor running.

The thief stepped into the gangway between two buildings and in shadow opened his knife in case they resisted. He felt his skin crawl and jerked around instinctively.

There stood George, head fully on, pasty like a dead man. He said drolly, "Don't steal."

Without warning, the thief lashed out at the visage with his razor-sharp blade. George's head predictably wobbled off, only this time it twisted, so it landed against his chest, facing out.

Surprised by looking down past his nose and up at the upside-down criminal's shocked face, George suddenly realized that the position was perfect, exactly what he'd been looking for.

"How do I look? Is it creepy?" he gushed.

Back against the wall, shocked by the apparition's dangling, talking head, the thief slashed at it again and again, to no avail. They stood glaring at each other. George's eyes strained to look down, or rather up, at the horror-stricken man.

"I'll take that as a maybe. Listen, I know we have a weak relationship so far, but I want you to know *I do look up to you.*" He hoped for a laugh, thought the line was funny, given the circumstances. But the thief wondered what was happening. Knife-in-hand, heart racing, he bolted toward the running car.

The unsuspecting family had just entered their home as the thief arrived. He flung the door open, jumped behind the wheel, and pulled the gear into Drive. A deteriorated hand appeared, covered the thief's hand, and pushed the shifter back into Park. The thief screamed at the sight of George wagging his finger from the passenger seat. His upside-down head shook back and forth.

"Naughty boy," he said.

The thief leaped out of the car and ran screaming down the street. Just to make sure he left the neighborhood, George trotted alongside him, his head flopping and flapping and grinning, explaining a criminal's life expectancy and sanity in Tower Grove East. He sang a throaty version of Nirvana's song, "Stay Away."

The thief summarily dispatched, George returned to his intersection. He felt exceptionally proud of his new maneuver. He had even delighted the twins. For once in a very long time, George eagerly awaited his next assignment.

5 TRACK LOVE TERROR

Overnight, sickly little Steven Bitaman became a super athlete. His stardom on every team left his classmates in the dust of envy, at least for one year. Some say his meteoric rise and ultimate end were a deal made with the Devil. Not quite.

The horror that unfolded began the first day of Steven's junior year at Roosevelt High, a school tucked into a corner of the Tower Grove East neighborhood of South St. Louis. He'd hated the last five high schools he got kicked out of, and he would hate Roosevelt, too. In fact, he hated everybody, which is why he felt fine cheating, lying, and stealing.

His mother and father worked the counter at a greasy spoon

downtown and dropped him off at Gravois and Compton at 5:50 AM. Right away he took to walking Roosevelt's quarter-mile track around the football field to feel as though he was going somewhere, even if it exhausted him.

One morning, he heard something behind him and turned to look. A girl appeared out of nowhere. Her hair cut ragged, dirt on her face, she stood staring at him.

He kept walking, then stopped to look at her again. She had vanished. He turned back around, and there she was in front of him. Her abrupt appearance stopped him dead in his tracks.

"What . . . do you want?" he asked.

"You," she said. "I have watched you since you first came to walk around and around, and you seem so lonely." The apparition gestured toward the enormous oak tree beyond the track in the field's corner and said, "My grave is deep below that tree." She peered into his eyes and slowly said, "I have watched thousands since they built this school upon our graveyard and have felt nothing—until I saw you."

Steve realized he felt a strange attraction, too. He perhaps recognized her from a dream. He smiled.

"I'm Steven," he said and put his hand out. She looked at it, then faded and disappeared. Steven was not sure if what had just happened really happened. The first rays of light in the September sky lanced the field. Certain his imagination had gotten the better of him, he shakily went to the bleachers to sit till the school opened.

The next morning at the track, he saw the girl at the other end of the field. A warm breeze relaxed him, and he walked toward her. She waited. He sped up without thinking, wanting to get closer to her, to hear her voice again. She vanished. Then she was next to him. He kept walking; she stayed at his side, her moccasins scraping the track. She did this for many mornings. No matter the weather, she would silently walk at his side, crunching the cinder in unison with him. Over time, they conversed in a most sublime and loving way, and each day, Steven grew more robust, more confident, stronger, and less evil.

He spent every minute of every morning before school, lunch breaks, after school, evenings, and holidays with her at the track where she urged him to become a superior athlete. They would speak of the two of them together forever in eternal love.

The others used to call him "rat boy," but not now. Steven stopped seeing people as enemies. He was, he thought, more blissful than any teenager had ever been.

Then one day, with graduation only a month away and the biggest track meet of his career minutes away, Steven was a bundle of nervous energy as he walked toward the track through adoring fans. He could not see her, but imagined her in the oak tree, watching him with pride from afar.

She observed Steven, her thoughts on what it would be like when his life left him, and they would abide happily together forever in the giant oak.

Caught up in the enormity, excitement, and inevitability of his coming triumph, an excited cheerleader took him by surprise, threw her arms around his neck, and kissed him. The kiss lasted longer than either of them had intended. The girl let go, then faded into the crowd. Steven realized what that kiss must have looked like to his beloved from the oak.

He broke free of the crowd and sprinted toward his spirited love to explain.

The unthinkable kiss pushed aside her love and enraged her.

She glared at him; her eyes filled with death. He had betrayed her.

Everyone watched in wonder as Steven abruptly stopped at the far end of the track and argued with the air. He held up his arms in self-defense against nothing as a scream escaped from him.

She tore at him, trying to scratch the kiss from his flesh. With a venomous, blazing hatred, she wanted him dead—now. For the first time, he saw her not as his sweet love and savior, but as a demon straight out of hell.

Steven fled from the apparition. Faster and faster, he ran on the inside lane counterclockwise. She chased him, and he ran like a maniac, unaware the opposing teams, officials, coaches, and fans stared in disbelief. With each yard he ran, he lost muscle and sinew. No one dared risk intervening in his macabre run of horror. The crowd of hundreds heard only the crunching sound of feet on the track and Steven's whimpers of terror. Until he collapsed.

The ambulance drivers tried to revive him. Frankly, his body, deflated like a collapsed balloon, unnerved them. The autopsy showed his heart had burst. A stronger athlete might have survived the horrendous trial, but given the sickly condition of the corpse, he had no chance.

On full moon midnights in Tower Grove East, one can witness—high in the dark branches of the giant oak at the corner of the Roosevelt's field—an unworldly, odious shaking just before dawn.

6 GNOME SWEET GNOME

Her eyes, dark with fury, followed the words across the computer screen as she typed, “To whoever stole my stone gargoyle statue from the front of my house. It stood guard over my home, here in Tower Grove East, for three years:” She paused, heart pounding. She glared at the screen, her anger boiling. Continuing, she wrote: “I declare it cursed now. May it come alive this night. May it hunt your thieving soul with such a rage it puts other gargoyles to shame.”

The gargoyle thief, a robust, unpleasant woman named

Edwina Swill, stood enduring her third public transportation transfer since she captured the stone statue. Edwina stared out the Metro window, thinking of all the gnomes trapped in the passing landscape. The St. Louis City limits sign drifted by as the train left the city. The gargoyle, wrapped in her coat, lay heavy on her lap. She looked at the bundle, not sure why she felt so compelled to steal it. Edwina *loved* gnomes, not gargoyles. She was loyal to the hundreds of gnomes she had rescued since beginning her crusade.

Her gnomes were now her family—growing their number was her only passion. Pointy hats, cheerful colors and white beards, her gnomes are always happy. They occupy all the space in her farmhouse. Yet, here on her lap is the only gargoyle she ever

"rescued". She didn't know why. Perhaps a vague notion of its being protective soothed her after nearly being caught. She sensed its power. She would use it to keep herself and the gnomes safe.

At the end of the line, Edwina exited the Metro. She lugged the heavy statue in her arms to her car in the commuter parking lot, set the bundle down and opened the trunk. Inside were the two gnomes she'd "collected" on her drive to the lot. She stroked their sweet faces, telling them they would be home soon, but that they must make room for a special new family member. Gnomes rearranged, she removed her coat from the gargoyle, hoisted it, and lay it between them.

She felt an unfamiliar presence and looked around to see what it was. She closed the trunk without noticing the startled faces of the gnomes inside.

The highway was empty and quiet. She breathed in the night air, smiled at the faint sound of crickets passing, when thumps sounded, and she swerved. Did the thud cause her to swerve or the other way around? She grimaced at the thought that she hadn't secured the stone gargoyle.

The car beams rolled with the winding country road, illuminating trees, shuttering her and her cargo against the moonless night. She turned in to a discreet gravel road, stopping at the gate with a large sign, "ROAD CLOSED," put there to insure her solitude and the safety of the gnomes. Key in the lock, she paused at an unfamiliar sound from behind the car. She walked over to see what it was. Nothing there.

Car through, she locked the gate behind her and then drove the long, wooded road onto her property. The national forest surrounded it on three sides. Tires rumbled over cattle guards and crunched gravel. She swerved and stopped at the front door of her cabin. The orange glow of the dusk-till-dawn light illuminated crowds of gnomes positioned to greet her or attend her departure. They, and she, happy in their seclusion.

Edwina smiled at her family in the yard, eager to introduce them and those inside to the newcomers. But before she unloaded, she had to make room for them, as newcomers always lived inside on arrival.

She opened the door and beheld her gnomes on the mantle, tables, counters, nightstands. The floor trembled as if hit with a half-second earthquake. Edwina, taken aback, sensed unseen danger. Then it dawned on her. Of course, now it made sense! She rescued the gargoyle by pure instinct to protect them all from whatever evil would be coming. So, she quickly cleared a spot in front of the fireplace, set down a ruby-red cloth, and surrounded it with candles—like a shrine. Edwina placed gnomes around for a ritual welcoming party and went outside.

Her eyes roamed the woods as she stepped into the sodium light. *Whatever it is, it's coming, if it isn't already here,* she thought. The gnomes surrounding the house in the dark and under the light seemed pensive. Or was it her? She opened the car's trunk to see the gargoyle lying sideways atop the remains of the crushed gnomes. Crestfallen, but not surprised, she bent to lift the gargoyle out, not seeing the upside down remains of a gnome skull, its half mouth in a full grimace.

She wiped away tears for the two lost gnomes. If only she had secured the stone statue. The gargoyle felt heavier as she lifted it out of the trunk to take its place as their guardian. She crossed the threshold; a shudder rippled through the house again, strong and moving the mass of gnomes backward, their eyes widening.

Gripped with a sudden fear, Edwina hurried to the shrine and set the gargoyle down, eager to be under its protection. The floor trembled again.

She leaned in closer to the gargoyle and sized it up. Didn't remember the savageness of its face, so different from her beloved gnomes. "Good!" she thought, "All the better to fend off evil."

Its eyes popped open, and its serrated teeth flashed. The lights blinked out, and her scream, heard only by terrified gnomes, abruptly died in the dark woods.

7 FIRE ALLEY

On the run and desperate, the robber saw his chance for easy cash step outside to lock the door to the bowling alley on the corner of Grand Boulevard and Juniata Street. He was on the manager before the poor fellow could react. A gun in the manager's ribs convinced him the crook got the drop on him—do nothing dumb.

The man ordered him to unlock the door and lock it again behind them. Then the robber pushed him up the broad red and white tiled steps. Grand Bowl occupied the entire second floor above the pizza parlor that had closed for the night.

Ordered to sit on the floor, the manager handed over his valise along with the keys, the weekend receipts, and a description of his car. Hefting a big black bowling ball, the robber let it drop on the manager's skull and rendered him dazed in a sprawl on the floor. The robber unzipped the valise and grinned at the wads of cash.

The manager groaned. His assailant stepped over him and headed for the cash register. Booze and snacks waited for him at the dark bar. He planned to get a gut full, dispose of the manager, and torch the joint. He'd dump the car on the East side and disappear on a Greyhound.

A whirring sound like something gearing up came from behind the rows of pins standing in the gloom of ten dark alleys: a hundred pale pins with a red stripe at their throats like open wounds. The manager groaned louder. He tried to get up, but the robber returned and dropped another ball on his head, silencing him.

A deep booming sound like a bowling ball hitting the hard maple floor in the center lane rumbled fast toward him for only a second… then nothing. His gut tensed with terror at the sudden quiet. No rolling, no gutter bump, no pins hit, no ball. Nothing but the manager's moans.

He spun around, extracting and pointing his snub-nosed thirty-eight every which way, poking it at the dark. His stomach rumbled. The jar of pickled eggs at the bar was just the ticket. It was the hunger what spooked him, made his imagination get all knotted up with whirrs and booms that didn't exist.

A pile of bowling shoes appeared out of nowhere, and he stumbled on them. He found his ankles twisting this way and that, as if the shoes were grabbing at him. He lost his footing, tumbled, and hit the floor hard. Out of pure frustration, he shot the right shoe of a men's 9-1/2.

Up and feet regained, he started for the bar again, but stopped short. A single pin that wasn't there before now stood on the floor in his path. He ran at it, kicked it hard, and broke his toe. He dropped his gun, fell hard again to the floor, and cradled his foot under a shower of cursing. The pin which flew into the dark never landed. No bangs, no bonks. The pain in his toe tangled with his hunger as he ran his hand across the floor in the darkness, trying to find his gun.

At the far end of the alley, the lights on an overhead score screen popped on over the ninth lane. The robber was sure someone else was in the place, and he bellowed, "Come out or I'll shoot!"

In the thick silence, his hand groped the floor in a futile search for the gun. Unable to find it, he got up and fearlessly limped to the bar and the eggs.

The overhead screen drew his attention when it went out.

Looking back at the jar of eggs, the sight of a nearby pin on the floor spooked him. He picked it up and threw it at the back bar, smashing a bottle of Cherry Liquor. But the pin stood erect on the shelf, its shoulders dripping red.

The robber grabbed two bottles of booze from the bar, his eyes riveted on the pin. He guzzled one and heaved the empty at the pin but missed. Then he snatched a bag of pretzels and stuffed his mouth. He glanced away from the pin and searched for the jar of eggs, while he opened the second bottle to steady his nerves.

Another overhead screen came on over the sixth lane and flickered, then screens three and one came on and flickered, too. He stared in amazement at the strobe of screens flashing; it made him dizzy, and he had to look away.

To his horror, the jar of eggs sat at the other end of the bar, and the pin he'd thrown the empty gin bottle at had vanished. He set his bottle down and gripped the bar rail. Unable to move, he stood watching the rest of the screens start flickering.

The pin racks dropped, picked up pins, and set them back down till all ten lanes with blinking screens and chomping racks seemed to come his way.

He shut his eyes and screamed. It all stopped. But not the sound of a slow-rolling ball growling across the floor, joined by another, which joined another and another, a thunder of a thousand invisible rolling, roiling bowling balls all coming at him from the darkness. He shut his eyes and screamed again. Then silence.

The robber opened his eyes to darkness. A *nothingness*. He grabbed the bottle and guzzled until it overflowed his mouth, soaking his face and shirt and coat. He let the empty drop, and he shoved his shaking hands into his coat, extracted his cigarettes and Zippo to light his coffin nail. Looked up, surprised to find in the glow of the lighter's flame, pins.

On every surface stood pins: on the bar, the floor, the chairs, the alleys, everywhere. Hundreds of bowling pins. He brought his hand to his heart in terror; the flame on his lighter ignited his alcohol-soaked clothes. Up he went, a screaming inferno.

The entire building burned to the ground that night. Passersby found the unconscious manager lying just outside the entrance, having no memory of what had occurred.

The place is a parking lot now. It is said that if you stand on the corner during big storms, you will hear a rolling thunder like no other. And sometimes, in the whipping wind's howl, you can hear a man—screaming.

8 MR. MEOWGI

Cecil Bacardi spun his moral compass as a gesture to his Christian youth, but it always landed askew on his need for the things of others. He was a professional burglar and a better-than-average safecracker. *To Catch a Thief* inspired him at every watching. He was no Cary Grant and had no Grace Kelly, nor was the city of St. Louis the French Riviera. Cecil fancied himself a sophisticate above rank amateurs that packed the city's jail.

He carried no weapons. The cops had never arrested him. They had no prints, no pictures, not even a parking ticket on him. He was an underwriter for an insurance company's unusual policies by day. Not the most lucrative or glamorous of professions, but it's not what you know, it's what you do with the knowledge.

Cecil used his access to identify potential targets, learn their security codes, safe types, and travel plans, and execute with precision each burglary. He had built up a small fortune to prepare for his early retirement on the French Riviera. He kept his thefts erratic, with long intervals and varying methods so as not to establish a pattern. What he wanted most was the ultimate score, one that would buy a first-class ticket to a first-class life. It came unexpectedly.

The flat above a small pet shop on the northeast corner of Arsenal and Michigan streets in the Tower Grove East neighborhood caught Cecil's attention. He'd been researching an unrelated matter and came upon a file. A note attached, brittle with age, referred to the appraisal of two twenty-five-pound bars of gold in a Bastet Safe Model 13 on the second floor. Cecil checked; the account was still active. The contract, over a hundred years old, never had a claim. A memorandum with it read, "Policy owner, Mr. Meowgi, recluse, no personal contact, attorney only."

Suppressing a smile, he searched police files for any history of trouble at the property: break-ins, an alarm system, anything. There was nothing. He couldn't believe his luck. The surveillance could get done over a few sick days. He decided he didn't feel so good.

He parked a block from the target and strolled by it. Just as he approached it, a screeching, escaped parakeet crapped on his shirt in a flyby. He stopped at the pet shop window, wiped away milky bird poo with his white handkerchief, and looked inside. The store, animated by caged pets, fell silent. A chill entered him, yet he left unruffled. Other than customers and deliveries, only an elderly woman came and went from the building—arriving at dawn and departing at sunset. Not once in his surveillance did anybody enter or exit the flat above, nor did lights come on. It had to be unoccupied (except for the Bastet Model 13).

When the day came, he parked on Arsenal at dusk and watched the old lady leave. He moseyed toward the door, carrying a bowling bag for the gold.

The adjoining store was quiet until he grabbed the doorknob. A parrot squawked inside the pet shop. Yapping, barking, and screeching erupted. He twisted pins in the lock, popped the door open, and entered the dark stairwell.

Cecil stood still until the animals next door quieted, then crept toward the stairs ascending the gloom. He froze. An orange tabby on the seventh step stared at him as its claws kneaded the stair tread. A parakeet perched on the next step up, stretched its wings out, and held them. Something brushed against his leg. The tabby now at his feet meowed at him. He kicked it, and the chorus of animals in the shop erupted again. The cat and bird disappeared. He shook it off and continued upward to seize his future.

When he reached the top, the red eyes of a trio of kittens startled him. Behind them, a crowd of cats surrounded the parakeet and tabby, and stared at him in silence, unmoving, in front of the Bastet 13. With each cautious step he took toward it, they backed away, forming a ring around their visitor.

He crept to the Goddess' 13, eying the silent animals

surrounding him. He checked the handle; it opened with ease. Alone in the dusty safe were the gold bars. He wasted no time and deposited them into the bag and turned to leave.

The number of house cats had increased at an alarming rate. So many. The tabby rose, stood erect, towering over the others, and faced him. Cecil's mind could not comprehend what was happening. He backed into the safe, leaning on its substance. He swung the bowling bag of bullion at the brindled queen. Cats swarmed out of shadows to attack his calves, driving razor fangs into muscle, tearing flesh, buckling knees; the rest converged on his body, teeth slashing, claws ripping. All in silence.

Cecil struggled against the surge, lurched to get up, to escape to sanity, to safety. The feeling in his legs gone, he crawled in desperation, his dripping flesh flayed open with jagged gashes. At the top of the stairs, the attack stopped. Heavy jaws snared his neck and dragged his limp, savaged body back, dropping their prize at the tabby's feet. An innumerable menagerie of silent cats now stood erect around him, like blood-soaked meerkats. On the wall hung a large, gold-framed portrait of the tabby. Its big brass plate said: Mr. Meowgi. Eyes wild with comprehension, he faded as crimson humor drained from his wounds like the warm waters of the French Riviera.

Key in hand, the elderly woman glanced in wonder at the shredded remains of a bowling bag in the gutter. The parakeet alit her shoulder. Mr. Meowgi nuzzled her with affection. She smiled sweetly and opened for business.

9 GRAFF-EATY

DAcey liked it when the cops called him a hard case. He had exploited his "bad" attitude. Since fifth grade. He considered himself a winner because of it, because people left him alone to brood about being mostly alone. When alone in his teens, he had created his graffiti alter ego and became its sub rosa spokesman. He traded in drugs under its banner, expanding and defending territory through his graffiti to intimidate and extort; they feared his mark. Some believed it could damn entire neighborhoods.

With graffiti in his veins, he considered himself a warrior in an ancient order with the sacred purpose of using graffiti as an engine of commerce. It didn't matter what era, what location, or method the artist used. From spray paint to marker to the sharp edge of a stone, or a fingertip dipped in blood, same, same. A million years ago, or yesterday, in every urban culture, LA—New York City—the Berlin Wall; primitive Aboriginal etchings—to DAcey, none of it was vandalism. Not a crime. Just a culture of territory, people. Simple assertive business, baby. Tags, throw-ups, and sales of dime bags. Someday he would put it all into a "piece," maybe a mural on the south leg of the Gateway Arch.

He was his graffiti.

It was after 10 PM, a good time to spread some marketing mayhem. As he steered the car, he shook spray paint cans and thought about what was on the menu of fear for the night. A gang sign—a racial slur—a threat, whatever.

On impulse, he made a left onto eastbound Shenandoah Avenue from Grand Boulevard into a neighborhood unfamiliar to him. Two blocks later, he saw a school, smiled, and circled the block. He would start his campaign there, saying to himself, "I'm about to assert some business all over this place."

He pulled up his black hoodie and got out when movement down the block caught his eye. People were leaving a building behind the school and passing a big yard sign: "Tower Grove East NEIGHBORHOOD MEETING TONIGHT." Perfect.

Not only would he mark fresh territory by announcing his presence to the kids in the school, but he would put the fear into the adults, too. He watched the people get into cars and houses and smirked at how he was about to shatter their sense of safety. He'd have them tamed in no time. A little fear helped the medicine go down . . . and made business go boom. It always did. While he waited, he listened to heavy metal on his headphones, selected and shook cans of spray paint before putting them into his backpack.

No people were around. The street was quiet. He pulled his backpack from the passenger seat, checked the rearview, scanned the street, slipped out the door. Slung the pack over his shoulder and headed to the shadows to do the neighborhood sign first.

At the sign, he glanced around and extracted a can from his backpack. He pointed and painted a blood red spray at the letters across Tower Grove East till a thick line bloomed and dripped. DAcey curved the spray down, then whipped up left like a leaning check mark across to the right. Then he superimposed his XXX. The tag was unmistakable. He turned to leave but stopped.

The paint was not there.

He shook the can and sprayed again. Again, it was there… then not. Another shot, another fast fade.

He wiped his finger on the sign where he'd just sprayed. Nothing on his finger. His fingertip tingled, then burned. He threw the spray can to the ground and got another from his backpack, shook it quickly and tagged the sign again.

Again, it faded. It had to be the material from which they made the sign. Was it the paint? He sprayed the air, and a cloud of crimson engulfed him.

The skin on his forearm itched. He left the sign and moved toward the school as he'd planned. Leaving the defective cans of spray paint where they lay, he threw his backpack on, and an unexpected pain through his back and shoulder startled him. He kept moving.

In a dark corner of the school, he extracted another can and began his tag. Without warning, every muscle in his legs rippled like he had snakes under his skin.

The tag he'd started disappeared, just like on the sign. He thrust his arm straight out, determined to finish, but then an itch on his arm became unbearable. He pulled his sleeve up and gaped, watching a crimson web under his skin form his triple X. Seized by an otherworldly ache clawing its way up his spine, he fell against the wall. Every pore in his body screamed for salvation.

Numb to the world he once knew, scalded ego terrorized, a cataclysm of fear and anger descended on DAcey. He bolted for his car deep in the inky night. Before he could get to his car, he dropped to the sidewalk, unable to breathe, felled by excruciating pain moving up his throat. Had to get to his car, had to get help, couldn't scream. Got up, stumbled forward. His head felt on fire.

He reached his car, grabbed the side mirror, and swiveled it to his face. Every tag he had ever done clawed its way out from his insides. They ate his flesh. They bloomed and welled on his hands and legs, face, tongue. Then he saw his eyes.

Bubbling up into his eyeballs the rune of the Osage, an even more ancient order, the one defending Tower Grove East with sacred purpose.

10 SAVAGE LITTER

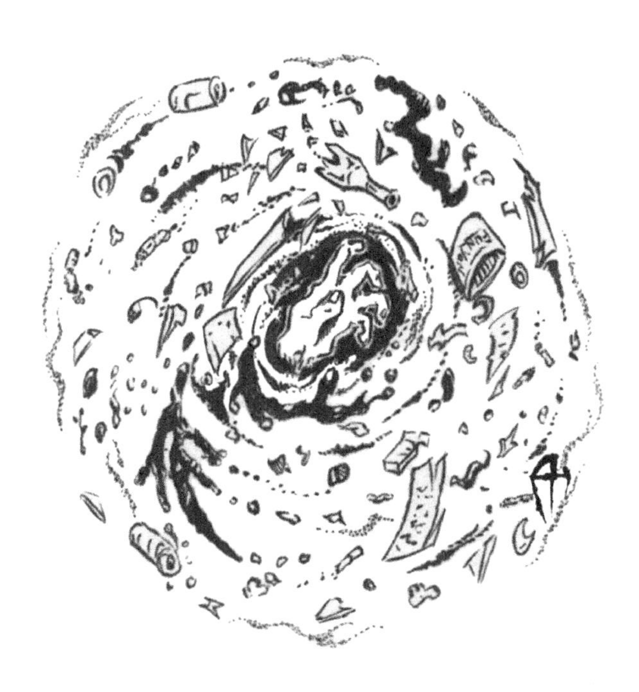

Susan was angry most of the time. She let people know she did not care about their little worlds, and they should stay the hell out of hers. The St. Louis Arch at her back, she sped south on Gravois Avenue and chomped so hard into a fried chicken leg the bone broke. She gnawed on the pieces as she turned right onto Wyoming Street into Tower Grove East 20 MPH over the limit, flipping the bones out the window. She blew through a stop sign. Vacuumed up the last drops of her 32-ounce soda and threw the cup out the window, scattering its lid, straw, and ice on the pavement like an arrow pointing her way.

Parallel parking was not what Susan wanted to be dealing with and proved it by banging the cars in back and front of her space. She snatched the full ashtray from the console, opened the driver's door, and banged the tray on the asphalt till it emptied out. Another stripped, splintered chicken bone fell from her lap. She tossed the ashtray on the passenger seat and grabbed her purse and the newspaper with the address for her appointment with a potential landlord to look the place over. A bottle tumbled from her car before she could close the door. She kicked it to the curb. It shattered.

Susan launched her half-smoked cigarette, crossed the street, pulled a stick of gum from her purse, ripped the paper off with her teeth, and blew it to the sidewalk. She stopped, checked the address against the one in her folded newspaper. It was the last possibility after a long day of looking at crumby places. At the right location now, she threw the newspaper onto a manicured lawn next door and headed up the steps. She stood staring at a sign taped to the door with her name on it, apologizing for missing the appointment because of an emergency and asking to reschedule. She spat her gum at the note.

Up to her ears with excuses, she pulled out her cigarette pack and shook it. One left, one damn cigarette that wouldn't come out. She ripped open the pack, leaving a flurry of paper, cellophane, and foil fluttering around her feet. The world was lucky her last match worked. Over the porch rail went the match and empty pack as she drew deeply, deciding what to do.

She settled on a walk to Grand Boulevard. Maybe get a little something-something to eat. Outside the door to the gas station, she flicked away her cigarette and searched the junk in her purse for the ten-dollar bill that would get her a pack of cigs and some food. A receipt agitated her, so she plucked it out and threw it away, along with a parking stub and a partially used Kleenex. The ten was on the bottom.

Shopping done, she walked to the corner, stopping at a trashcan with a green figure asking not to litter. Huffing at the sign, she set her bag of purchases on the edge of the receptacle. Pulled the items out and let the yellow smiley-face plastic bag drop onto the sidewalk. Off came the thin plastic strip and top of the cigarette pack that floated to the ground. She struck a match. A passing bus blew it out. So, she threw the matchstick at the public transport as its engine roar receded.

She smoked and thought about her choices as she devoured the contents of the green and yellow foil bag of Funyuns before she dropped it. The wind grabbed it, floated and flipped it, dropped and lifted it high above her. It gently fluttered and alit Susan's shoulder. She slapped it off, angered at having the filthy thing touch her.

Burned down to the filter, she flicked the still-lit butt into the trashcan, then popped the tab on her soda. Not wanting to return to her home on wheels, she stripped the Payday candy bar packaging halfway and bit down. The gathering dark and sudden chill motivated her, and she pulled her purse from atop the trash can to return to her car. She dropped the drained can in the gutter, finished the candy bar, threw its crumpled wrapper, and dug for another cigarette.

The Boulevard behind her, she paused on the sidewalk next to her car and stood there absentmindedly smoking. Something tickled her ankle; she looked down. The breeze held a swarm of litter against her foot.

She kicked them, took a last drag from her cigarette, tossed it, and walked toward the driver's door. A wad of sidewalk gum pulled her shoe off. She stumbled; stepped on a smashed aluminum can, its sharp point puncturing her exposed toe.

She screeched and bent to look for blood when pain exploded on her other foot. The cigarette butt she'd flicked blew back. It landed on the patch of skin between the top shoe straps of her other foot. She screamed and thrashed.

Susan struggled against the wind to get up. She stepped on the slick Funyuns bag lying on the grass. Down she went, again. The plastic bag's big smiley yellow dot slapped onto her face. She swatted and punched at it. Confused, she rolled into the gutter, and shattered glass gathered into her armpits as she flailed. The broken chicken bone pierced her thigh.

She rolled in agony. A bent straw entered her ear. On hands and knees, bloodied and terrified, she crawled to the car door. The wind packed her ears, eyes, and mouth with the contents of the ashtray she'd emptied. A paper cut from the parking stub slashed across her throat. A hellish swirl of her own litter pulled hard until her hand tore from the door. The detritus of her life returning in a horrific, insane, matricidal whirlwind savaging her for offending the sanctuary of the Tower Grove East neighborhood.

11 SOUL BOXING

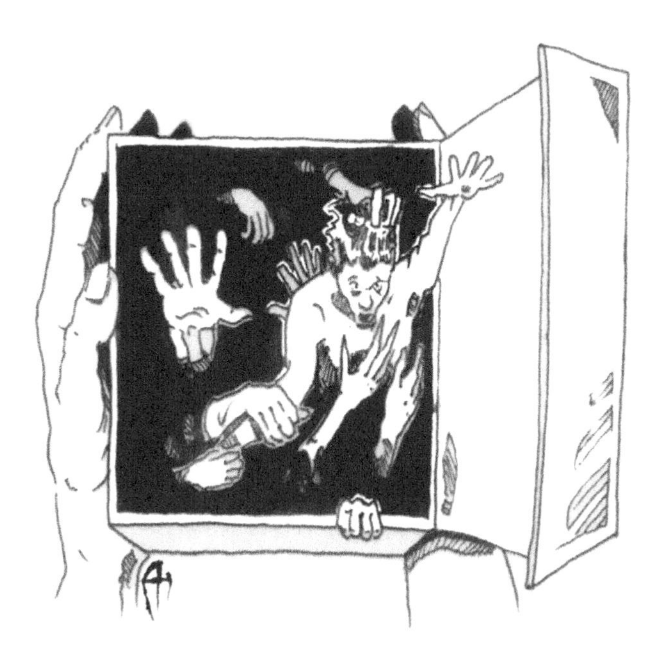

Detective Haugh of the St. Louis Police Department paid little attention to the news. He sat at his home desk sipping his morning coffee, scanning through ComStats on his laptop. What happened during the few hours he'd slept?

For the hundredth time, he looked for dots to connect. He selected all fields of crime statistics over the last six months in the city limits involving parole violators. A growing number had gone missing.

The TV weather report warned of flooding along with continuing downpour. He sipped and fast forwarded. They had assigned a color to each type of crime. Assaults, burglaries, larceny, domestic disputes, etc. appeared on the city-wide map in waves and bursts. Something caught his eye. He replayed it again and again. Within the carnival of colored dots, there appeared an opening in the gray dots of low-level crime. Package theft had dropped dramatically in TGE over the same time period as his parolees became missing persons. Made no sense.

Sammy became a teenager the day he met Big Ray, his sister's boyfriend. Sammy wanted to be Big Ray. All he had to do is what he was told. Ray had it down. He'd follow the first delivery truck he saw. He'd eyeball what the driver put on porches and between doors without knocking or ringing the bell. Then, he'd circle the block and park out of view of security cameras. Next, send Sammy to snatch the box and toss it in the trunk. And repeat the process until the trunk and back seat were full. He'd fence the goods from his garage. When finished, he'd go through a roll of money like it was candy. By dawn, he'd be broke.

Above the roar of the storm, he shouted at the door, "I'm Detective Haugh, ma'am, St. Louis police department." The woman pulled the curtain aside and looked the rain drenched young redhead up and down. She thought him young for a detective, but he had the badge.

She let the curtain fall back and cracked the door open two inches. "What do you want?"

"Ma'am, I am trying to find some missing people. Would you look at a few photos on the chance you might recognize any of them?"

The assumption that she would know anything of such matters took her aback. She minded her own business, kept to her neighbors, and knew nothing of strangers. "Why are you asking me?"

"We are asking everyone, Ma'am. Do you mind?" He presented his laptop, slowly scrolled through the photos, and watched her eyes. She looked at a dozen photos of disgruntled looking young men, then shook her head no.

The cold heat of futility rippled over Detective Haugh's face. He shut the device and asked, "Have you had any packages stolen lately?"

"Well, Lisa across the street asked me to keep an eye out for a delivery last week. They stole her package anyway. I couldn't spend all day standing at the window. Talk to her." She gave him a look, then closed the door. Why on earth, she wondered, didn't she say something to Lisa, or the detective? Why didn't she tell them that the man on Lisa's porch holding a strange box literally vanished? And she just now saw him in the last photo the detective showed her.

Ray said the thunderstorm dumped so much rain it was good cover. Sammy didn't mind. He got too much of a thrill from the heist to worry about getting wet. This was the big time.

It was like sitting under a waterfall. The traffic light turned red. A big dark step van glided through its green light. Ray made a right on red and followed it into TGE. The truck blinkered a right turn and halfway down the block stopped. They watched the driver exit the truck with a small package. He walked purposely through the downpour to the porch and dropped the box without knocking or ringing. Then drove off into the torrent like a ghost ship sailing off the end of the world.

The car jerked to a stop. "Get to it," Ray said, and Sammy bolted to the porch. Ray moved his eyes between the rear-view and side mirrors, straight ahead and at the porch. He saw Sammy bend to pick it up. Then nothing. Ray stared at the spot, no sign of Sammy. He stopped short of blowing the horn. What the hell could he be doing? Still no Sammy. The tension made him nervous. He cussed at Sammy through the closed window.

A car approached. Ray was double parked. Had no choice and had to move. He circled the block over and over, searching for the idiot. He expected him to be walking down the street with the box. After he had enough, he double parked again, threw his hoodie over his head, and walked through the downpour.

He stepped right up and onto the porch. No Sammy. Only the box. Ray glared at it for the longest time as the roar of the storm filled his ears. The urge to touch the box overcame him, but his long-practiced instinct as a thief stood the hair on his neck up. He paused and peered through the late afternoon light and deluge.

The trees hung heavy over dark cars and houses. Something was happening. Something wasn't right. The entire neighborhood felt crouched around him, ready to spring. He needed to get out, but not without the package.

The instant he picked it up, the lid opened. Inside, being pulled down by other doomed package thieves, was a terrified Sammy screeching, "RAY! HELP ME!" Ray, seized by horror, vanished quietly along with the box.

12 OWL GET YOU

Three times, Max faced death. The third time death got lucky . . . and paid the price.

Max grew up in the rolling foothills of the Ozarks. He worked in the family vineyard alongside his parents, where he developed a kinship with spirits of all kinds. His slight limp came from a tractor rollover; his first encounter with mortality at age eleven. The second time, his Uncle Thomas fell over drunk into the pond and nearly drowned Max, who dove in to save him and then needed saving himself. That was his second run-in with the reaper.

City folk came to the Ozarks in the fall of every year for harvest. Max enjoyed the city folk, even those that couldn't hold their wine. With them, he could engage in his favorite activity: listening to and talking to just about everybody, about everything. When there were no humans around, he would begin chatting up critters in the surrounding hills.

Max could mimic birdcalls to a point of conversation. His favorite and longest relationship was with a Barred Owl that lived in the trees around his home. They grew up together, and Max felt looked out for each other. Many a night, his Pa would threaten the switch if he didn't stop their sleep-disturbing back and forth, "Who cooks for you? Who cooks for y'all? Who?"

When Max reached twenty-one, he told his parents he wanted to move to the city. His Uncle Thomas said he would hold a place for him should he ever want to return. His Ma gave him a steel owl to mark the occasion. "To keep you company and remind you to be civil," she said. His father bequeathed Max his bowler should the need arise.

Max's parents were certain he would thrive anywhere, even in the wilds of the city. His Uncle Thomas, faced with a booming post-prohibition business, believed his nephew's decision providential. Before long, Max was slinging drinks at the Tick Tock Tavern in the Tower Grove East neighborhood of South St. Louis. He kept that owl his Ma gave him on a shelf across from the bar where he could see it. On afternoons before the regulars arrived and nights after closing, he would taunt the mute bird, urging it to answer, "WHO?"

The first day on the job and every day thereafter, Max wore his father's bowler. He grew a thick, black handlebar mustache over his ever-present, pudgy smile, just like his father. Max thought about his time at the Tick Tock, among hundreds of friends that flowed in and out like the tide. It was as close to heaven as he'd likely get. Max became the guardian of the Tick Tock and the neighborhood, for he was by all accounts a civil man.

It was Tuesday, the slowest night of the week, as evidenced by the last customer saying goodnight. Uncle Thomas had gone home, and Max figured a quick dispatching of his duties would get him to his room for a radio show and a ham on rye. Max hooted at his steel owl, "Who cooks for you!" Then, just as the clock on the bar struck midnight, the door burst open.

In came a breathless woman Max recognized from the neighborhood, scared out of her wits, running away from the door screaming, "He's coming! Please! Help me!" Then the door slammed open again. A stranger came into the Tick Tock. Max looked away from the woman and at an enormous, dark visage.

Evil came from it in waves. Still behind the bar, Max turned to the woman, now struck silent with terror, pointed, and said, "The toilet is that way, Miss. Go in and lock it."

Max was not a tall man by any measure. He carried his powerful frame like a wrestler to come around from behind the bar. The monster towered over him and snarled. Dark embers flared in its eyes. Max kept moving and in a steely voice said, "We are closed Mr." A deep, menacing growl came from the behemoth. "Rudeness is an act of fear, my friend," Max said in a steady voice, "you are safe here, as long as you're civil."

The beast mimicked Max's movements toward the woman, still frozen where she stood. Max considered the creature far from civil. So, on his way to meet his tough customer up close, he reached beneath the bar and grabbed the nightstick his Uncle Thomas kept there. In a swift maneuver, Max urged the woman toward the toilet, then turned to do what he must in the name of civility.

Focused and ready to pounce on Max, a shrill question voiced from behind the creature startled and distracted it. "Who cooks for you!" Without hesitation, much to the monster's dismay, Max attacked.

The woman, feet braced against the toilet, back against the door, felt the pressure of the battle between good and evil vibrate on her spine; the horror of the struggle punctuated by howling and screeching and the furious flapping of metal wings. Palms pressed hard against her ears, she opened her mouth, and her scream became the maelstrom's chorus.

Max's Uncle Thomas arrived the next morning and found the door open. Alarm swept over him. He peered in. The room was in order except for a few lights his nephew should have turned off. The faint sound of sobbing drew him to the ladies' room, where he found the woman.

They never found Max, nor heard from him again. His disappearance and the incomprehensible story the woman told devastated Uncle Thomas. He kept Max's owl on the mantle across from the bar where it still sits in silent vigil.

Outside, above the door, hangs a portrait of Max, as a reminder to all who enter Tower Grove East—be civil.

13 THE GOBBLEDYGOOK

On the odd occasion, children of Tower Groove East are called to gather on a Halloween night . . . to save the world. With great anticipation, they convene before a black crate in shadow. Through its top, facing the children, in horrifying crimson, the letters *AH AH AH* scratched all the way through.

Lights behind and in front of the crate gradually come up, revealing a hooded figure nearby. She bows deeply then speaks softly, "Good evening, Tower Grove East children. Thank you for answering the call to save your world once again. As Queen of the Night, Empress of Lore, and keeper of Gobbledygook stories, I must ask, Are you ready?" A sea of solemn heads bob in silent assent.

"But first, are there any children here that know how to laugh?" All hands go up. She then asks for volunteers to demonstrate their laughter. After the demonstrations, the Queen of the Night stares at the children without a word for a long time.

Speaking slowly, she says, "Boys and girls, teens, moms and dads, all of us, we all laugh at things that are funny, don't we? Sometimes we laugh at a friend being silly or a dog chasing its tail. Laughter makes us feel better; it is one of the most enjoyable human things to do. It IS important. Perhaps . . . even more important than you think."

The Queen of the Night for the first time turns to the dark box and walks over to it, tipping it back slowly so the cryptic red letters roll backwards to the top, out of view. A large warning label now facing them says, *DANGER! - GOBBLEDYGOOK! - DO NOT OPEN!* Above the label is a big latch and pin.

She pauses, points at the crowd around her, and says, "Before this night is done, goodness will be restored. Get close and listen to the air as I tell you of . . ." She pulls the pin, grabs the lid suddenly, and growls, "The Gobbledygook."

The Queen of the Night holds her hands in the air to still the gasps. "Stay calm. I assure you it is safe. The Gobbledygook is not in there, at least not yet.

"Allow me to remind you what The Gobbledygook is. It has been among mankind from the beginning of time, warned of in ancient stories on every continent, a relic of evil continually needing containment. This, its empty coffin, proves it is loose again. When it gets out to feed, it is hard to recognize until it is too late.

"It is said that anyone who sees The Gobbledygook as it really is will immediately go potty in their pants." Reacting to the giggles of surprise from the children, she goes on, "That is funny, but to be so scared that *that* happens? That is the opposite of funny: it is terrifying.

"The earliest written proof of the Gobbledygook and its coffin is in the Dead Sea Scrolls. The most famous, in the late seventeen hundreds, is the tale of a ship lost at sea. A ship that didn't sink because of a storm or an accident, not because it sprang a leak, or went down in a tsunami, but because unknown to the crew, there was a stowaway . . . The Gobbledygook.

"Its coffin, discovered in the ship's hold by an unfortunate sailor, who opened it. All went mad, instantly dooming the ship.

"Only the captain of the ship survived the horror. In the madness to keep body and soul together, he found he could not destroy it, but he discovered how to return it to its grim coffin, to which he clung as his ship and crew sank into the gloom. No one knows how long he floated alone with the vile beast, its casket his ghastly life preserver.

"It floated ashore with him on its back. Once pulled onto the beach, the captain, with his dying breath, repeated a crazy laugh over and over, nodding at what he'd scratched into the coffin, then dying before revealing anything more. Those who found him had to pry his body off the box, hooked there by bloody fingernails that had dug through the wood to make a message no one understood.

"The dark box and its darker inhabitant disappeared. But throughout history, in times of great unhappiness, there are signs the Gobbledygook is feeding on humans again. Infamous, horrible, mean characters and all sorts of terrible people throughout history that made civilization miserable had succumbed to Gobbledygook. This is why every time it gets out; we must put it back again.

"The Gobbledygook is a despicable monster. It won't bite you in half or swallow you whole. It survives by eating you from the inside. It enters your ears, fills your brains, then controls your eyes, your tongue, and finally your heart.

"When the monster has its fill, it leaves its human buffet looking exactly the same, but unable to speak truth or common sense and loses good intention. The victims are easily swayed by nonsense and everything they say with all sincerity is . . . gobbledygook.

"Why am I telling you this? Why is The Gobbledygook's coffin here at my feet? Why!?" Opening the lid and tipping it forward she answers, "Because as you can see, is gone again! The Gobbledygook is out there in the dark right now, and it's coming this way, because it knows we have gathered. It is up to you, the children of Tower Grove East, on this most frightening of nights to capture it again.

"Don't be alarmed, even though the Gobbledygook is the most terrifyingly horrible, stinky, worst monster in the whole wide world, it is afraid of and controlled by only one . . . thing." The Queen of the Night closes the coffin lid, points to the crimson letters, and says, "This, the bloody message scratched into the coffin by the unfortunate captain. It is the secret to getting the Gobbledygook back in there and keeping it there." She rolls the box back, so the lid is on top again, then opens it. The light behind the box shines through the cuts in the lid and the letters are different.

"Look," the Queen of the Night says, pointing to it, "everybody thinks the scratched-in message is to be read from the outside. . ., but it's *not*. The message is meant to be seen from inside of the box . . . by the Gobbledygook. It doesn't say AH AH AH." It says, HA HA HA.

"It's not just any laugh: it's a secret laugh. One that terrifies the Gobbledygook, because when it hears the laugh, its ego must rush back into its coffin to survive. That is why we are here tonight. The Gobbledygook is on its way now, here, to your city. It knows I will tell you one of its stories of defeat and it wants to stop me. But we will stop it first.

"Now, we must practice the secret laugh if we are to survive this night. Repeat after me." In a slow, deliberate voice she says, "HA. HA. HA." After several group practices, she raises her hand for silence.

"I am closing its sarcophagus now, but when the moment arrives in this terrifying story, I will raise it again. When I do, you must all laugh exactly like we practiced. The future depends on it."

The Queen of the Night clears her throat, brings up her hood, and adjusts it on her shoulders, becoming the Empress of Lore, and says, "This story is of two children and their parents who learned the hard way how to recapture the Gobbledygook." After a dramatic pause, she tells the children their story.

A boy named Franky, and a girl named Jenny were brother and sister. Jenny was twelve and Franky was nine. Their parents were both archeologists. They specialized in ancient evil spirits and the talismans humans used to control them. Their parents were away a lot, but that's OK, because it was the modern world, the children could take care of themselves as they were taught. But sometimes things happen.

Franky, walking by his mother's office one day, thought he heard a noise come from inside, and given his mom and dad were not home, he stopped to listen at the door. There it was again, very faint. He opened the door and stepped into the room, listening again, but couldn't hear anything.

A whisper brushed his ear. He turned, pinning its source on a black box that sat upon the floor in front of his mother's desk with a notebook on top. He hadn't turned on the lights and could see it in the reflected light from the hallway. He listened again. Nothing. He examined the box when Jenny, passing through the hall, saw her mother's door open and looked in.

"Franky!" said Jenny after seeing what he was doing. "You are NOT supposed to be in there. You know that."

"I think I hear something coming from inside," Franky said, pointing at the black box with big white and red letters on it: *DANGER! - GOBBLEDYGOOK! - DO NOT OPEN!*

"Oh, no, no, no. You know the rules, we are never to touch anything. Ever. Get away from there. Come on, get out." She pointed to the door and waited for her younger brother to leave.

He silently walked into the hallway and asked as she closed the door, "Have you ever heard of a Gobbledygook?"

She shook her head. "If you are so curious, look it up." With that, she turned and continued down the hallway to her room.

Jenny sat at her desk. Franky had gotten his iPad, and leaning on her door frame, read aloud, "Says it is an informal noun. *A letter or speech full of legal gobbledygook*: gibberish, claptrap, nonsense, rubbish, balderdash, blather, garbage; mumbo jumbo, drivel, tripe, hogwash, baloney, bilge, bullshit, bunk, poppycock, phooey, hooey . . ."

Jenny, trying to concentrate on her homework, yelled at Franky, "Will you please stop! I get it. It means nonsense, talking without saying anything. Whatever."

"I don't get it," Franky said. "It sounds stupid. Why is that dangerous?" He shrugged and added, "Adults are afraid of the weirdest things."

"Uh, hello, that's because they have experience," said Jenny. "Now go away. I have to get my homework done before mom and dad get home." She put on her headphones and turned the volume up.

Franky tried to imagine what was in the box as there was no picture nor mention of it being evil or monstrous. He wondered what it looked like and why it was making those noises. "Fine." he said to an unhearing Jenny and went directly to his mother's office, sneaked in, and closed the door behind him.

Enough light came in from around the window to outline the dark box on the floor. Franky approached it and touched it. It trembled. He jerked his hand back at the unexpected movement. Then a tiny voice inside seemed to whimper and cry, then fall silent. Franky thought it must be afraid, whatever it was. He put his hand on the notebook atop the box. This time, the trembling was unmistakable. He stroked the side of the box and heard a sigh.

Franky, sure it was harmless and small, heard what sounded like a giggle. He lifted the notebook off the top and tucked it under his arm. Dim light revealed crazy scratching on the top. He found a crude latch and pin on the front and partially removed the pin. The box trembled again. He looked at the door, hesitating, then thought there was nothing to worry about and pulled the pin out the rest of the way.

The lid flew open, Franky fell backwards, something dark streaked out and crashed into the bookcase. Books exploded off the shelves, furniture overturned, papers fell like confetti, then the thing darted into the shadow beneath the desk where it stopped abruptly.

On the floor and startled, Franky could hear its heavy breathing right in front of him. He slowly crab-crawled backward to get away and to the door. He shot up and ran. His fingertips touched the knob. Something heavy and furious climbed onto his back. He twirled around and around, bashed into a table, knocking it and a lamp onto the floor before spinning into an overstuffed chair, then onto the floor, rolling back and forth until the thing flew from his back. Franky screamed, "Jenny! Jenny, help me! Jenny!

Jenny, at her desk and focusing on geometry, didn't hear the struggle, only the beat of the music filling her ears.

Franky, on all fours, his back against a closet on the other side of the room, was now ten feet from the door. He didn't want to scream again, trying to be still. Sweat fell into his eyelash and dripped onto what he was leaning on. He looked closer: it was the notebook. It had to have the answer for what to do. He sensed the thing coming from his left and instinctively opened the door to the closet behind him to slip in and close behind him. Before he could close the door, whatever it was, hit the door and slammed it shut. Franky pulled at the handle to keep it shut with one hand, held the notebook tight with the other and started kicking the walls and screaming!

Jenny heard something and felt a thumping. She pulled off her headset and got up to go see. As soon as she got in the hallway, she could hear Franky screaming and pounding. Her heart raced as she ran toward his room but stopped. There it was again, coming from their mom's office.

She threw the door open and turned on the light. revealing her mother's office, turned upside down. She screamed, "Franky!" The lights went out. The door slammed shut. Jenny's feet shot out from under her. Something dragged her toward her mother's desk. She screamed in terror, "HEEEEEEEELP!"

Franky dropped the book and burst out of the closet and ran to help Jenny. He grabbed her hands and pulled as she screamed, "What is happening? Help me!"

The thing let go, and they both fell away. It moved between shadows to the closed hallway door, its heavy breathing the only sound. Franky whispered in Jenny's ears, "We have to run to the closet." Jenny nodded yes. They charged into the open closet and pulled the door closed behind them. The Gobbledygook hit the door hard, rattling the hinges.

His mind racing, Franky felt around for the notebook. He was sure the answer to stopping the Gobbledygook was in it. As soon as he found it, he realized the closet didn't have a light, and it was too dark to read. "Jenny, your phone! Do you have your phone?!"

Jenny shakily stretched her leg out in the crowded, dark closet to get her phone asking in a harsh, quick whisper, "What is going on, Franky? What did you do? What is that? What's happening?"

Jenny's phone lit the closet. She pulled up contacts to call her mom. Franky snatched the phone away. "Wait. We're safe in here." He held up the notebook and said, "I have this."

The Gobbledygook boomed against the door, making coats

drop and boxes fall off shelves. "Just give me a minute to figure this out. If mom and dad come, they will need this notebook, but we have it. What if they can't come in to save us without it? This is my fault and I want to fix it." Jenny just stared in silent acceptance as her little brother read every word with great intensity while the beast pounded the door at her side.

Franky closed the old volume slowly and said, "There is only one way to stop it. All present must speak aloud something carved through the top of the box that can only be read when it's open. It's the only way to get that thing back into the box."

The Gobbledygook bumped hard against the door more furiously than before. Jenny said, "I'm not going back out there!" She tried to snatch the phone from Franky and said, "I'm calling dad!"

Franky held tight to the phone and pleaded, "Please! It's the only way to keep everybody safe. We will be OK. This is my fault. Help me fix it and I'll never snitch on you again."

"Right," said Jenny. "Fine. What is your plan?"

"The box is in front of mom's desk. I'll run out first and go to the right to draw it toward me. You run to the box, open the lid, and use your phone light to shine through the open lid so I can read what it says inside. I'll tell you and we say it slowly together, no matter what. You got it?"

The Gobbledygook hovered outside the door, waiting to feed. Franky rushed out, hitting the dark creature, making it roll backward. Jenny headed for its coffin.

The Gobbledygook jumped up, leaped onto Franky's head and tried to get into his ear.

Jenny saw what was happening and stopped to grab a pillow from the floor. She threw it, knocking her brother down and the

Gobbledygook into the corner. Franky scrambled to his feet. Jenny got behind the box and tried to pull the pin out of the clasp. Her fingers fumbled. They could hear it scrambling around in the shadows, back-and-forth-back-and-forth. Jenny shouted at Franky, "The clasp! The clasp, I can't open it!" She turned to the noise behind her.

Franky got to the box, lifted the clasp, and popped open the lid. Before she could shine the light, the Gobbledygook pulled Jenny under the desk. She screeched and kicked until her heel hit it hard. It let go and went for Franky.

Jenny held her phone up, its light shining through the lid. Franky dodged the monster, focusing on the letters, and said to himself, "HA HA HA". Jenny screamed at him as the Gobbledygook raised up behind him to strike, "Franky! What is it?! What does it say?!

Franky screamed, "It's HA HA HA! Say it!" They repeated it, but it did nothing. The Gobbledygook was on Franky the instant he remembered and yelled, "All present must say it together! We are not saying together! Do it now!" Franky screamed.

The Empress of Lore stops reading, lays down the book, her eyes looking up at unseen forces. She points in the air, her hand tracing something swooping down on them. In a harsh whisper, she says, "It's here! The Gobbledygook is here! The story has summoned it."

Holding her free hand high, she opens the lid, light shining through its cuts revealing its secret message. The Empress of Lore shouts in a full and powerful voice reminiscent of Franky's instruction, "We must say it together. We must . . . do it . . .

now!"

Her hand drops, and in unison with the children the slow laughter begins: HA. HA. HA. Black clouds streaked with the deep red of willful ignorance boil overhead. A hot wind swirls past children and violently collides with the box.

At that precise moment, the Empress of Lore slams the box shut and pushes the pin in.

Adjusting her hood back up, The Queen of the Night opens her arms and declares, "Well done, children of Tower Grove East! You've done it again! Happy Halloween, everyone!"

ACKNOWLEDGEMENTS

My undead appreciation to Sarah Truckey, Judith Rubin, Joey Michaud, Gidget Frischer, David Hollingsworth, and Mary Schirmer for proof of their editorial input.

Illustrative of a fun partner in a cool collaboration, Alan Hollingsworth's inky imagination brings a malevolent style to horrify horror.

Writing and drawings do not a book make. My great appreciation goes to Dennis Fleming. His creative input turned a macabre idea into a menacing book. He then convinced his alter ego, renaissance publisher, and pseudonym Andy Ashling, to give it bat wings and unleash it on the world.

It's their fault it's out there now.

Special thanks to Adina, my lifelong partner and mother of our children, for continuing to softly close the door when I get that look in my eye to write.

Finally, to Sofia, Liam, and Emma Grace, you inspire me. I loved that the Gobbledygook came from you, proving my grandchildren are weirder than me.

All proceeds from the sale of this book go to creating and celebrating public art in the Tower Grove East Neighborhood.

—W. F. G.

Made in the USA
Middletown, DE
21 October 2022